Brayan's Gold

Brayan's Gold

PETER V. BRETT

Subterranean Press 2011

First Edition

ISBN
978-1-59606-363-1

Subterranean Press
PO Box 190106
Burton, MI 48519

www.subterraneanpress.com

For Matt

Raised on a steady diet of fantasy novels, comic books, and Dungeons & Dragons, Peter V. Brett has been writing fantasy stories for as long as he can remember. He received a bachelor of arts degree in English literature and art history from the University at Buffalo in 1995, then spent more than a decade in pharmaceutical publishing before returning to his bliss. He lives in Brooklyn with his wife, daughter, and an evil cat named Jinx. You can visit Peter on the web at www.petervbrett.com

Other books by Peter V. Brett

The Warded Man

The Great Bazaar

The Desert Spear

Introduction

IT'S all Matt's fault.

Seriously. This novella probably wouldn't exist had not my friend and longtime beta-reader, Matt Bergin, demanded it.

He had been reading an early draft of *The Great Bazaar*, and in it, I have Arlen reference one of his past misadventures where he encounters a snow demon without having the proper wards to protect himself.

"When did Arlen meet a snow demon?" Matt asked. "Did I miss that story?"

"There's no story," I said. "I just like reminding people that Arlen had a ton of adventures back when he was young and working for the Messenger's Guild."

"Well, you've gotta write it, now," Matt said.

"Why?" I asked. I kind of liked the cryptic reference.

"Dude," Matt said. "You're passing up a chance to write about snow demons?"

It was a compelling argument, but I was swamped and couldn't get to it. I put the idea aside for over a year, but that whole time, I kept thinking about damned snow demons, and knew I would soon have poor Arlen's teeth chattering.

In the short break I allowed myself between finishing *The Desert Spear* and formally starting *The Daylight War*, I wrote this story, *Brayan's Gold*, the second stand-alone tale set in the world of the Demon Cycle.

I really enjoy this format, as it gives me a chance to tell short adventure stories that don't fit into the larger novels, offering newcomers an introduction to the series and some of its characters, longtime readers a broader look at the world, and impatient fans a coreling fix in the long wait between novel publications. Subterranean Press has been amazing in helping share these tales in beautiful limited edition books that feel as personal to me as the stories themselves.

This volume is extra special, because in addition to the story, it has a cover illustration and interior art by the incredibly talented Lauren K. Cannon (www.navate. com), who has been designing wards and doing paintings for my website ever since I first sold *The Warded Man* back in 2007. Lauren has done an amazing job of bringing my characters and symbol magic to life, and it was a pleasure to work with her again on this project.

So if you are a newcomer or an old friend, welcome. I hope you enjoy *Brayan's Gold*.

And if you don't...blame Matt.

Peter V. Brett
August, 2010
www.petervbrett.com

324AR

H O L D still," Cob grunted as he adjusted the armor.

"Ent easy when a steel plate's cutting into your thigh," Arlen said.

It was a cool morning, dawn still an hour away, but Arlen was already sweating profusely in the new armor— solid plates of hammered steel linked at the joints by rivets and fine interlocking rings. Beneath, he wore a quilted jacket and pants to keep the plates from digging into his skin, but it was scant protection when Cob tightened the rings.

"All the more reason to make sure I get this right, Cob said. "The better the fit, the less likely that will happen when you're running from a coreling on the road. A Messenger needs to be quick."

"Don't see how I'll be anything near quick wrapped in bedquilt and carrying seventy pounds of steel on my back," Arlen said. "And this corespawned thing's hot as firespit."

"You'll be glad for the warmth on the windy trails to the Duke's Mines," Cob advised.

Arlen shook his head and lifted his heavy arm to look at the plates where he had painstakingly fluted wards into the steel with a tiny hammer and chisel. The symbols of protection were powerful enough to turn most any demon blow, but as much as he felt protected by the armor, he also felt imprisoned by it.

"Five hundred suns," he said wistfully. That was how much the armorer had charged—and taken months in the making. It was enough gold to make Arlen the second-richest man in Tibbet's Brook, the town where he had grown up.

"You don't go cheap on things that might mean your life," Cob said. He was a veteran Messenger, and spoke from experience. "When it comes to armor, you find the best smithy in town, order the strongest they've got, and bugger the cost."

He pointed a finger at Arlen. "And always…"

"…ward it yourself," Arlen finished with his master, nodding patiently. "I know. You've told me a thousand times."

"I'll tell it to you ten thousand more, if that's how long it takes to etch it into your thick skull." Cob picked up the heavy helmet and dropped it over Arlen's head. The inside was layered in quilt as well, and it fit him snugly. Cob rapped his knuckles hard against the metal, but Arlen heard it more than he felt it.

"Curk say which mine you're off to?" Cob asked. As an apprentice, Arlen was only allowed to travel on guild business accompanied by a licensed Messenger. The guild had assigned him to Curk, an aging and often drunk Messenger who tended to work only short runs.

"Euchor's coal," Arlen said. "Two nights travel." Thus far, he had only made day-trips with Curk. This was to be the first run where they would have to lay out their portable warding circles to fend off the corelings as they slept by the road.

"Two nights is plenty, your first time," Cob said.

Arlen snorted. "I stayed out longer than that when I was twelve."

"And came out of that trip with over a yard of Ragen's thread holding you together, I recall," Cob noted. "Don't go getting swollen because you got lucky once. Any Messenger alive will tell you to stay out at night when you *have* to, not because you *want* to. The ones that want to always end up cored."

Arlen nodded, though even that felt a little dishonest, because they both knew he *did* want to. Even after all these years, there was something he knew he needed to prove. To himself, and to the night.

"I want to see the higher mines," he said, which was true enough. "They say you can look out over the whole world from their height."

Cob nodded. "Won't lie to you Arlen. If there's a more beautiful sight than that, I've never seen it. Makes even the Damaji Palaces of Krasia pale."

"They say the higher mines are haunted by snow demons," Arlen said. "With scales so cold your spit will crack when it hits them."

Cob grunted. "The thin air is getting to the folks up there. I Messaged to those mines a dozen times at least, and never once saw a snow demon, or heard tale of one that bore scrutiny."

Arlen shrugged. "Doesn't mean they're not out there. I read in the Library that they keep to the peaks, where the snow stays year round."

"I've warned you about putting too much faith in the Library, Arlen," Cob said. "Most of those books were written before the Return, when folks thought demons were just ale stories and felt free to make up whatever nonsense they saw fit."

"Ale stories or no, we wouldn't have rediscovered wards and survived the Return without them," Arlen said. "So where's the harm in watching out for snow demons?"

"Best to be safe," Cob agreed. "Be sure to look out for talking Nightwolves and fairy pipkins, as well."

Arlen scowled, but Cob's laugh was infectious, and he soon found himself joining in.

When the last armor strap was cinched, Arlen turned to look in the polished metal mirror on the shop's wall. He was impressive looking in the new armor, there could be no doubt of that, but while Arlen had hoped to cut a dashing figure, he looked more like a hulking metal demon. The effect was only slightly lessened when Cob threw a thick cloak over his shoulders.

"Keep it pulled tight as you ride the mountain path," the old Warder advised. "It'll take the glare off the armor, and keep the wind from cutting through the joints."

Arlen nodded.

"And listen to Messenger Curk," Cob said. Arlen smiled patiently.

"Except when he tells you something that I taught you better," Cob amended. Arlen barked a laugh.

"It's a promise," he said.

They looked at each other for long moments, not knowing whether to clasp hands or hug. After a moment they both grunted and turned away, Arlen for the door and Cob for his workbench. Arlen looked back when he reached the door, and met Cob's eyes again.

"Come back in one piece," Cob ordered.

"Yes, Master," Arlen said, and stepped out into the pre-dawn light.

ARLEN WATCHED THE great square in front of the Messengers' Guildhouse as men argued with merchants and stocked wagons. Mothers moved about with their chalked slates, witnessing and accounting the transactions. It was a place pulsing with life and activity, and Arlen loved it.

He glanced at the great clock over the Guildhouse doors, its hands telling the year, month, day, and hour, down to the minute. There was another great clock at the Guildhouse in every Free City, all of them set to the Tender's Almanac, which gave the times of sunrise and sunset for the coming week that were chalked beneath the clock face. Messengers were taught to live by those clocks. Punctuality, or better yet early arrival, was a point of pride.

But Curk was always late. Patience had never been one of Arlen's virtues, but now, with the open road beckoning, the wait seemed interminable. His heart thudded in his chest and his muscles knotted with excitement. It had been years since he last slept unprotected by warded walls, but he had not forgotten what it was like. Air had never tasted so good as it had on the open road, nor had he ever felt so alive. So free.

At last, there was a weary stomp of booted feet, and Arlen knew from the smell of ale that Curk had arrived before he even turned to the man.

Messenger Curk was clad in beaten armor of boiled leather, painted with reasonably fresh wards. Not as strong as Arlen's fluted steel, but a good deal lighter and more flexible. His bald pate was ringed by long blond hair streaked with gray, which fell in greasy gnarls around a weathered face. His beard was thick and roughly cropped, matted like his hair. He had a dented shield strapped to his back and a worn spear in his hand.

Curk stopped to regard Arlen's shining new armor and shield, and his eyes took a covetous gleam for an instant. He covered it with a derisive snort.

"Fancy suit for an apprentice." He poked his spear into Arlen's breastplate. "Most Messengers need to *earn* their armor, but not Master Cob's apprentice, it seems."

Arlen batted the speartip aside, but not before he heard it scratch the surface he had spent countless hours polishing. Memories came to him unbidden: the flame demon he struck from his mother's back as a boy, and the long cold night they spent in the mud of an animal pen as the demons danced about testing the wards for a weakness. Of the night he had accidentally cut the arm from a fifteen foot tall rock demon, and the enmity it bore him to this day.

He balled a fist, putting it under Curk's hooked nose. "What I done or not ent your business, Curk. Touch my armor again and the sun as my witness, you'll be spitting teeth."

Curk narrowed his eyes. He was bigger than Arlen, but Arlen was young and strong and sober. Perhaps that was why he stepped back after a moment and nodded an apology. Or perhaps it was because he was more afraid of losing the strong back of an apprentice Messenger when it came time to load and unload the carts.

"Din't mean nothin' by it," Curk grumbled, "but you ent gonna be much of a Messenger if you're afraid to get your armor scratched. Now lift your feet. Guildmaster wants to see us before we go. Sooner we get that done, sooner we can be on the road."

Arlen forgot his irritation in an instant, following Curk into the Guildhouse. A clerk ushered them right into Guildmaster Malcum's office, a large chamber cluttered with tables, maps, and slates. A former Messenger himself, the guildmaster had lost an eye and part of his face to the corelings, but he continued to Message for years after the injury. His hair was graying now, but he was still a powerfully built man, and not one to cross lightly. A wave of his pen could bring dawn or dusk to a Messenger's career, or crush the fortune of a great house. The guildmaster was at his desk, signing what seemed an endless stack of forms.

"You'll have to excuse me if I keep signing while we talk," Malcum said. "If I stop even for an instant, the pile doubles in size. Have a seat. Drink?" he gestured to a crystal decanter on the edge of his desk. It was filled with an amber liquid, and there were glasses besides.

Curk's eyes lit up. "Don't mind if I do." He poured a glass and threw it back, grimacing as he filled another near to the rim before taking his seat.

"Your trip to Duke's Coal is postponed," Malcum said. "I have a more pressing assignment for you."

Curk looked down at the crystal glass in his hand, and his eyes narrowed. "Where to?"

"Count Brayan's Gold," Malcum said, his eyes still on the papers. Arlen's heart leapt. Brayan's Gold was the most remote mining town in the duchy. Ten nights' travel from the city proper, it was the sole mine on the third mountain to the west, and higher up than any other.

"That's Sandar's run," Curk protested.

Malcum blotted the ink on a form, turning it over onto a growing stack. His pen darted to dip in the inkwell. "It was, but Sandar fell off his ripping horse yesterday. Leg's broke."

"Corespawn it," Curk muttered. He drank half his glass in one gulp and shook his head. "Send someone else. I'm too old to spend weeks on end freezing my arse off and gasping for breath in the thin air."

"No one else is available on short notice," Malcum said, continuing to sign and blot.

Curk shrugged. "Then Count Brayan will have to wait."

"The count is offering one thousand gold suns for the job," Malcum said.

Both Curk and Arlen gaped. A thousand suns was a fortune for any Message run.

"What's the claw?" Curk asked suspiciously. "What do they need so badly it can't wait?"

Malcum's hands finally stopped moving, and he looked up. "Thundersticks. A cartload."

Curk shook his head. "Ohhh, no!" He downed the rest of his glass and thumped it on the guildmaster's desk.

Thundersticks, Arlen thought, digesting the word. He had read of them in the Duke's Library, though the books containing their exact composition had been forbidden. Unlike most other flamework, thundersticks could be set off by impact as well as spark, and in the mountains, an accidental blast could cause an avalanche even if the explosion itself didn't kill.

"You want a rush job, carrying thundersticks?" Curk asked incredulously. "What's the corespawned hurry?"

"Spring caravan came back with a message from Baron Talor reporting a new vein; one they need to blast into," Malcum said. "Brayan's had his Herb Gatherers working day and night making thundersticks ever since.

Every day that vein goes uncracked, Brayan's clerks tally up the gold he's losing, and he gets the shakes."

"So he sends a lone man up trails full of bandits who will do most anything to get their hands on a cartload of thundersticks." Curk shook his head. "Blown to bits or robbed and left for the corelings. Hardly know which is worse."

"Nonsense," Malcum said. "Sandar made thunderstick runs all the time. No one will know what you're carrying save us three and Brayan himself. Without guards, no one seeing you pass will think you're carrying anything worth stealing."

Curk's grimace did not lessen. "Twelve hundred suns," Malcum said. "You ever seen that much gold in one place, Curk? I'm tempted to squeeze into my old armor and do it myself."

"I'll be happy to sit at your desk and sign papers, you want one last run," Curk said.

Malcum smiled, but it was the look of a man losing patience. "Fifteen, and not a copper light more. I know you need the money, Curk. Half the taverns in the city won't serve you unless you've got coin in hand, and the other half will take your coin and say you owe a hundred more before they'll tap a keg. You'd be a fool to refuse this job."

"A fool, ay, but I'll be alive," Curk said. "There's always good money in carrying thundersticks because sometimes carriers end up in pieces. I'm too old for demonshit like that."

"Too old is right," Malcum said, and Curk started in surprise. "How many message runs you got left in you, Curk? I've seen the way you rub your joints in bad weather. Think about it. Fifteen hundred suns in your accounts before you even leave the city. Keep away from the harlots and dice that empty Sandar's purse, and you could retire on that. Drink yourself into oblivion."

Curk growled, and Arlen thought the guildmaster might have pushed him too far, but Malcum had the look of a predator sensing the kill. He took a key from his pocket and unlocked a drawer in his desk, pulling out a leather purse that gave a heavy clink.

"Fifteen hundred in the bank," he said, "plus fifty in gold to settle your accounts with whichever creditor is lingering by your horse today, looking to catch you before you leave."

Curk groaned, but he took the purse.

THEY HITCHED THEIR horses to Brayan's cart, but in Messenger style, kept them saddled and packed in addition to the yoke. They might require speed if a wheel cracked close to dusk.

The cart looked like any other, but a hidden steel suspension absorbed the bumps and depressions of the road with nary a jostle to the passengers and cargo, keeping the volatile thundersticks steady. Arlen hung his head over the edge to look at the mechanics as they rode.

"Quit that," Curk snapped. "Might as well wave a sign we're carrying thundersticks."

"Sorry," Arlen said, straightening. "Just curious."

Curk grunted. "Royals all ride around town in fancy carts suspended like this. Wouldn't do for some well-bred Lady to ruffle her silk petticoats over a bump in the road, now would it?"

Arlen nodded and sat back, breathing deeply of the mountain air as he looked over the Milnese plain spread out far below. Even in his heavy armor, he felt lighter as the city walls receded into the distance behind them. Curk, however, grew increasingly agitated, casting suspicious eyes over everyone they passed and stroking the haft of his spear, lying in easy reach.

"There really bandits in these hills?" Arlen asked.

Curk shrugged. "Sometimes mine townies short on one thing or another get desperate, and *everyone* is short on thundersticks. Just one of the corespawned things can save a week's labor, and costs more than townies see in a year. Word gets out what we're carryin', every miner in the mountains will be tempted to tie a cloth across his nose."

"Good thing no one knows," Arlen said, dropping a hand to his own spear.

But despite their sudden doubt, the first day passed without event. Arlen began to relax as they moved past the main roads miners used and headed into less traveled territory. When the sun began to droop low in the sky, they reached a common campsite, a ring of boulders painted with great wards encircling an area big enough to accommodate a caravan. They pulled up and unhitched the cart, hobbling the horses and checking the wards, clearing dirt and debris from the stones and touching up the paint where necessary.

After their wards were secure, Arlen went to one of the firepits and laid kindling. He pulled a match from the drybox in his belt pouch and flicked the white tip with his thumbnail, setting it alight with a pop.

Matches were expensive, but common enough in Miln and standard supply for Messengers. In Tibbet's Brook where Arlen was raised, though, they had been rare and coveted, saved only for emergencies. Only Hog who owned the General Store—and half the Brook—could afford to light his pipe with matches. Arlen still got a little thrill every time he struck one.

He soon had a comfortable fire blazing, and pan fried some vegetables and sausage while Curk sat with his head propped against his saddle, pulling from a clay jug that smelled more like an Herb Gatherer's disinfectant than anything fit for human consumption. By the time they had eaten it was full dark and the rising had begun.

Mist seeped from invisible pores in the ground, reeking and foul, slowly coalescing into harsh demonic form. There were no flame demons in the cold mountain heights, but wind demons materialized in plenty, as did a few squat rock demons—no bigger than a large man, but weighing thrice as much, all of it corded muscle under thick slate armor. Their wide snouts held hundreds of teeth, bunched close like nails in a box. Wood demons stalked the night as well, taller than the rock demons at ten feet, but thinner, with barklike armor and branch-like arms.

The demons quickly caught sight of their campfire and shrieked in delight, launching themselves at the men and horses. Silver magic spiderwebbed through the air as the corelings reached the wards, throwing the force of the demons' attack back at them and knocking more than a few to the ground.

But the demons didn't stop there. They began to circle, striking at the forbidding again and again as they searched for a gap in the field of protection.

Arlen stood close to the wards without shield or spear, trusting in the strength of the magic. He held a stick of graphite and his journal, taking notes and making sketches as he studied the corelings in the flashes of wardlight.

Eventually, the corelings tired of their attempts and went off in search of easier prey. The wind demons spread their great leathery wings and took to the sky, and the wood demons vanished into the trees. The rock demons

lumbered off like living avalanches. The night grew quiet, and without the light of the flaring wards, darkness closed in around their campfire.

"Finally," Curk grunted, "we can get some sleep." He was already wrapped in his blankets, but now he corked his jug and closed his eyes.

"Wouldn't count on that," Arlen said, standing at the edge of the firelight and looking back the way they had come. His ears strained, picking up a distant cry he knew too well.

Curk cracked an eye. "What's that supposed to mean?"

"There's a rock demon coming this way," Arlen said. "A big one. I can hear it."

Curk tilted his head, listening as the demon keened again. He snorted. "That demon's miles from here, boy." He dropped his head back down and snuggling into his blankets.

"Don't matter," Arlen said. "It's got my scent."

Curk snorted, eyes still closed. "*Your* scent? What, you owe it money?"

Arlen chuckled. "Something like that."

Soon, the ground began to tremble, and then outright shake as the gigantic one-armed rock demon bounded into view.

Curk opened his eyes. "That is one big ripping rock." Indeed, One Arm was as tall as three of the rock demons they had seen earlier. Even the stump of its right arm, severed at the elbow, was longer than a man was tall. One Arm had followed Arlen ever since he had crippled it, and Arlen knew it would continue to do so until one of them was dead.

But it won't be me, he promised the demon silently as their eyes met. *If I do nothing else before I die, I will find a way to kill you.*

He raised his hands and clapped at it, his customary greeting. The coreling's roar split the night, and darkness vanished as the powerful demon struck hard at the ward-net with its talons. Magic flared bright and strong, throwing the demon back, but it only spun, launching its heavy, armored tail into the wards. Again the magic rebounded the blow. Arlen knew the shock of magic was causing the demon agonizing pain, but One Arm did not hesitate as it lowered its spearlike horns and charged the wards, causing a blinding flash of magic.

The demon shrieked in frustration and came again, circling and attacking with talon, horn, and tail, in its search for a weakness, even smashing the stump of its crippled arm against the wardnet.

"It'll tire out and quit the racket soon enough," Curk grunted and rolled over, throwing the blanket over his head.

But One Arm continued to circle, hammering at the wards over and over until the wardlight seemed perpetual, the flashes of darkness like eye blinks. Arlen studied the demon in the illumination, looking for a weakness, but there was nothing.

Finally Curk sat up. "What in the Core is the matter with that crazy..." His eyes widened as he caught a clear look at One Arm. "That's the demon from the breach last year. The one-armed rock that stalks Jongleur Keerin for crippling it."

"Ent after Keerin," Arlen said. "It's after me."

"Why would it..." Curk began, but then his eyes widened in recognition.

"You're him," Curk said. "The boy from Keerin's song. The one he saved that night."

Arlen snorted. "Keerin couldn't save his own breeches from a soiling if he was out in the naked night."

Curk chuckled. "You expect me to believe you're the one that cut that monster's arm off? Demonshit."

Arlen knew he shouldn't care what Curk thought, but even after all these years, it grated on him that Keerin, a proven coward, had taken credit for his deed. He turned back to the demon and spat, his wad of phlegm striking the coreling's thigh. One Arm's rage quadrupled. It shrieked in impotent fury, hammering even harder at the wards.

All the color drained from Curk's face. "You crazy boy, provoking a rock demon?"

"Demon was already provoked," Arlen pointed out. "I'm just showing it's personal."

Curk cursed, throwing aside his blankets and reaching for his jug. "Last run I do with you, boy. Never get to sleep now."

Arlen ignored him, continuing to stare at One Arm. Hatred and revulsion swirled around him like a cloud of stink as he tried to imagine a way to kill the demon. He had never seen nor heard of anything that could pierce a rock demon's armor. It was only an accident of magic that severed the demon's arm, and not something Arlen would bet his life on the odds of repeating.

He looked back at the cart. "Would a thunderstick kill it, you think? They're meant to break rocks."

"Them sticks ent toys, you crazy little bugger," Curk snapped. "They can do ya worsen any rock demon. And even if you've got a night wish and want to try anyway, they ent ours. If they count sticks and it don't meet the tally that left Miln, even by one, it's worse for our reputation than if we lost the lot."

"Just wondering," Arlen said, though he cast a longing look at the cart.

It WAS QUIET the next day, as they rode across the southern base of Mount Royal—the western sister of Mount Miln—whose eastern facing was filled with small mining towns. But the number of signposts dwindled as they made their way to the western face, and the road became little more than wagon ruts leading a path through the wilderness, with a few rare forks.

Late in the day, they reached the point where Royal joined with the next mountain in the range, and there stood a great clearing surrounding a gigantic wardpost made of crete, standing twenty feet high. The wards were so large a whole caravan could succor underneath them.

"Amazing," Arlen said. "Must've cost a fortune to have that cast and hauled out here."

"A fortune to us is just copper lights to Count Brayan," Curk said.

Arlen hopped down from the cart and went over to inspect the great post, noting the hard way the dirt in the clearing was packed, indentations telling the tale of hundreds of firepits and stakes put down by Messengers, caravan crews, and settlers over the years. The site was freshly used even now, smelling faintly of woodsmoke from a previous night's fire.

As he studied the wardpost, Arlen noticed a brass plaque riveted into the base of the post. It read: *Brayan's Mount.*

"Count Brayan owns the whole mountain?" Arlen asked.

Curk nodded. "When Brayan asked permission to mine all the way out here, the Duke laughed and gave him the whole damn mountain for a Jongleur's song. Euchor didn't know that Countess Mother Cera, Brayan's wife, had found tale of a gold mine on the peak in an old history."

"Reckon he's not laughing now," Arlen said.

Curk snorted. "Now Brayan owns half the crown's debt, and Mother Cera's arse is the only one in the city Euchor's afraid to pinch." They both laughed as Arlen began to climb the post, clearing windblown leaves and even a fresh bird's nest from the wards.

It was a cold spring night, but the post radiated heat, drawn from the demons that attempted to breach its radius. The forbidding waned the further one got from the post, but it easily extended fifty feet in every direction. Even One Arm could not approach.

The next morning, they began to ascend the winding road that would twist around the entire mountain three times, getting ever narrower, rockier, and colder, before it brought them to Brayan's mine. It was around midday when they approached a large rock outcropping, and a shrill whistle cut the air. Arlen looked up just as something struck the bench between him and Curk, blasting through the wood like a rock demon's talon.

"That was just a sign to let you know we mean business," a man said, stepping out from around the rock face. He wore thick coveralls and a miner's helm with candle cup. A kerchief was tied across his nose to cover the rest of his face. "Fella atop them boulders can thread a needle with his crank bow."

Arlen and Curk glanced up and saw there was indeed a man kneeling atop the rocks, his face similarly covered as he pointed a heavy crank bow at them. A spent bow lay at his side.

"Corespawn it," Curk spat. "Knew this would happen." He lifted his hands high.

"He only has one shot," Arlen murmured.

"One's all he needs," Curk muttered back. "Crank bow this close'll go through even your fancy armor like it was made of snow."

They turned their eyes back to the man on the road. He carried no weapons, though he was followed by two men with hunter's bows nocked and drawn, and they by half a dozen thick-armed men with miner's picks. All wore the candled helms with kerchiefs across their faces.

"Ent lookin' to shoot anyone," the bandit leader said. "We ent corelings, just men with families to feed. Everyone knows you Messengers get paid in advance and keep your own bags on your horses. You unhitch that cart and go on about your business. We ent looking to take what's yours."

"I dunno," said one of the men with picks, as he strode up to where Arlen sat. "Might need to take that shiny warded armor, too." He tapped Arlen's breastplate with his weapon, putting a second scratch in the steel, next to the one Curk had made.

"The Core you will," Arlen said, grabbing the pick haft just under the head. He yanked it back and put his steel-shod boot in the face of the man as he was pulled forward. Teeth and blood arced through the air as the man hit the ground hard.

Arlen tossed the pick down the mountain and had his shield and spear out in an instant. "Only thing anyone comes near this cart will be taking is my spear in their eye."

"You crazy, boy?" Curk demanded, his hands still lifted. "Gonna get killed over a cart?"

"We promised to see this cart to Brayan's Gold," Arlen said loudly, never taking his eyes off the bandits, "and that's what we're going to do."

"This ent a game, boy," bandit leader said. "A crank bow bolt will punch right through that shield."

"Your bowman had best hope so," Arlen said, loud enough for the bowman to hear, "or we'll see if he can dodge a spear without falling off those rocks and breaking his neck."

The leader stepped up and grabbed the arm of the bandit Arlen had kicked, hauling him to his feet and shoving him back towards the others in one smooth motion.

"That one's an idiot," he told Arlen, "and he don't speak for us. I do. You keep your armor. We don't even need your cart. Just a few crates off the back, and we'll let you ride on safe and sound."

Arlen stepped into the back of the cart, putting his boot on a crate of thundersticks with a thump. "These crates? You want I should just kick 'em off the cart?"

Curk gave a shout and backpedaled, falling from his seat. Everyone jumped.

The leader held up his hand, patting the air. "No one's sayin' that. You know just what it is you're carryin', boy?"

"Oh, I know," Arlen said. He kept his shield up as he squatted, setting down his spear and pulling out a thunderstick. It was two inches in diameter and ten long, wrapped in a dull gray paper that belied the power within. A thin fuse of slow burning twine hung from one end.

"I've a match, to go with it," Arlen said, holding the thunderstick up for all to see.

The bandits on the ground all took several steps back. "You be careful now, boy," the leader said. "Them things don't always need a spark to go off. Ent wise, swingin' it around."

"Best keep your distance, then," Arlen said. For a moment, silence fell as he and the bandit leader locked stares. Then came a sudden snapping sound, and everyone jumped.

Arlen looked over to see that Curk had cut his horse from the cart harness and was swinging into the saddle. He readied his spear and shield, and turned to face the bandits. Arlen saw doubt in the bandit leader's eyes, and smiled.

But Curk kept his speartip down, and Arlen felt his momentary advantage vanish.

"Don't want no part of some thunderstick show-down!" Curk shouted. "I got years of drinking ahead of me, and fifteen hundred suns to pay for it!"

The bandit leader gave a start, but then he nodded. "Smart man." He signaled the others to move back, giving Curk an open path back down the road. "You stay smart, and keep on riding when you see the wardpost."

Curk looked at Arlen. "Can't handle a scratch on your armor, but you'll blow yourself to bits over a cart? You ent right in the head, boy." He kicked his horse hard, and in moments he had vanished back down the trail. Even the sound of his galloping hoofbeats quickly faded.

"Ent too late to do the same," the bandit leader said, turning back to Arlen. "You ever seen what a thunderstick can do to a man? What you've got in your hand'll blow you apart so there's nothing to burn at the funeral. Tear that pretty warded armor of yours like paper."

He gestured down the trail where Curk had ridden. "Get on your horse and go. You can even take that stick in your hand for insurance."

But Arlen made no move to get off the cart. "Who told you we were coming? Was it Sandar? If I find his leg ent really broken, I'll break it for him."

"Don't matter who told us," the bandit said. "No one's going to think you didn't do your duty. You done Messengers proud, but you ent gonna win this. What do you care, if Count Brayan sees a dip in his ledgers? He can afford it."

"Don't care about Count Brayan," Arlen admitted. "But I care about my promises, and I promised to get this cart and everything on it to his mines."

The men spread out, three picks and a bowman at either end of the road. "That ent gonna happen," the bandit leader said. "You try to move that cart, we shoot your horse."

Arlen glanced at the bowmen. "Shoot my horse and it'll be the last thing you ever do," he promised.

The bandit sighed. "So where does that get us, 'cept half hour closer to dark?"

"How close are you willing to get?" Arlen asked. He rapped his gauntlet against his scratched breastplate. "I'll stand here in my 'pretty warded armor' right until the rising."

He looked out over the bandits, all of them on foot and none carrying so much as a pack. "You, I expect, need to get on back to succor at Brayan's Wardpost before dark. That's why you told Curk to keep on riding, and it's at least five hours walk back the way we came. Wait too long, and you won't make it in time. Is it worth it to get cored over a few boxes of thundersticks when you have families to feed?"

"All right, we tried to do it easy," the bandit leader said. "Fed, shoot him." Arlen ducked under his shield, but there was no immediate impact.

"You said no names, Sandar!" the crank bowman cried.

"Ent gonna matter, you idiot, once you put a bolt through this head," Sandar snapped.

Arlen started. Of course. He had never met Sandar, but it made perfect sense. He shifted his shield so he could see the bandit. "You faked the break so you could ride out a day early and ambush your own shipment."

Sandar shrugged. "Ent like you're gonna live to tell anyone."

But still there was no shot from above. Arlen dared to peek over his shield. Fed's hands shook, his aim veering wildly, and finally he put up the weapon.

"Corespawn it, Fed!" Sandar shouted. "Shoot!"

"Suck a demon's teat!" Fed shouted back. "I didn't come out here to shoot some boy. My son's older'n him."

"Boy had his chance to walk away," Sandar said. Some of the others grunted in agreement, including the man Arlen had kicked.

"Don't care," Fed called. "'No one gets hurt', you said. 'Just a dip in some Royal's ledger.'" He pulled the bolt from his bow and slung the weapon over his shoulder, picking up the spare as well. "I'm done." He moved to pick his way down the outcropping.

One of the other bowmen eased his draw as well. "Fed's right. I'm sick of eatin' gruel as anyone, but I ent lookin' to kill over it."

Arlen looked for the last bowman's reaction, but the man only sighted and fired.

He got his shield up in time, but it was a heavy bow, and the shield was only a thin sheet of hammered steel riveted onto wood, meant more to defend against corelings and nightwolves than arrows. The arrowhead made it through before the shaft caught fast, puncturing the side of Arlen's cheek. He stumbled back and almost lost his balance, squeezing the thunderstick so hard he was afraid it would go off in his hand. Everyone tensed.

But Arlen caught himself and straightened, turning to reveal the match clutched in his shield hand. He struck it with his thumb, and it lit with a pop.

"I'm going to light the fuse before the match burns my finger," he said, waving the thunderstick, "and then I'm going to throw it at anyone still in my sight."

A couple of men turned and ran outright. Sandar's eyes narrowed, but at last he lifted his kerchief to spit, and whistled for the rest to follow him as he headed down the road.

The match did end up burning Arlen's hand, but he never needed to light the fuse. A few minutes later he was back on his way up the mountain. Dawn Runner was not pleased about pulling the entire load, but it could not be helped. He didn't think the bandits would be able to follow him on foot, but he kept the thunderstick and his drybox close to hand, just in case. It was nearing dark when he made it to the next wardpost.

Sandar was waiting.

THE MESSENGER HAD shed his miner's disguise, clad now in battered steel mail and carrying a heavy spear and shield. He sat atop a powerful destrier, much larger than a sleek courser like Dawn Runner. With a horse like that, and no cart to slow him or limit his path, it wasn't surprising that he had gotten ahead of Arlen.

"Had to be a goody, dincha?" Sandar asked. "Couldn't leave it alone. Guild is insured. You're insured. You could've ridden off with Curk. The only loser would have been Count Brayan, and that bastard's got gold comin' out his arse."

Arlen just looked at him.

"But now," Sandar raised his spear. "Now I *have* to kill you. Can't trust you to keep your mouth shut otherwise."

"Any reason I should?" Arlen asked. "I don't take kindly to having bows aimed at me." He picked up the thunderstick sitting next to him in the driver's seat.

Sandar moved his horse closer. "Do it," he dared. "Blast this close'll set off every crate. Kill us both, and the horses besides. Either way, them sticks ent getting to Brayan's Gold."

Arlen looked him hard in the eyes, knowing he was right. Whatever Curk might think, he wasn't crazy, and didn't want to die today.

"Then get off your horse," Arlen said. "Fight me fair, and our spears can decide which of us walks away."

"Ent no one can say you ent got stones, boy," Sandar laughed. "If you want me to hand you a proper beating before I kill you, I'll oblige." He rode into the clearing by the wardpost, dismounting and staking down his horse. Arlen followed and set the thunderstick down, taking up his spear and shield before hopping down from the cart.

He set his feet apart in a comfortable stance, his shield and spear ready. He had practiced spearfighting with Cob and Ragen for countless hours, but this was real. This time, it would end in blood.

Like most Messengers, Sandar was built more like a bear than a man. His arms and shoulders were thick, with a barrel chest and a heavy gut. He held his weapons like they were a part of him, and his eyes had the dead, predatory stare of One Arm. Arlen knew he would not hesitate on the killing stroke.

They began to circle in opposite directions, eyes searching for an opening. Sandar made an exploratory thrust of his spear, but Arlen batted it aside easily and returned quickly to guard, refusing to be baited. He returned a measured thrust of his own. As expected, Sandar's shield snapped up to intercept.

Again Sandar attacked, this time more forcefully, but the moves were all simple spear forms. Arlen knew all the counters and picked them by rote, waiting for the real attack, the one that would come as a surprise when he thought he was countering something else.

But that attack never came. Sandar was powerfully built and had murder in his eyes, but fought like a novice. After several minutes of dancing around the wardpost, Arlen tired of the game and stepped into the next predictable attack. He ducked, hooking Sandar's shield with his own and raising both to cover himself as he stomped on the side of the Messenger's knee.

There was a sharp snap that echoed in the crisp air, like the branch of a winter-stripped tree breaking off in the wind. Sandar screamed and collapsed to the ground.

"Son of the Core! You broke my ripping leg!" he howled.

"Promised I would," Arlen said.

"I'll kill you!" Sandar shrieked, writhing on the ground in agony.

Arlen took a step back and raised his visor. "I don't think so. Fight's over, Sandar. Sooner you realize that, the sooner I can come set that leg for you."

Sandar glared at him, but after a moment, he threw his spear and shield out of reach. Arlen put down his own weapons and took Sandar's spear. He braced it against the ground and snapped it with a sharp kick of his steel-shod heel. He laid the two halves on the ground by Sandar and knelt to examine the leg.

As he did, Sandar threw a fistful of loose dirt right in his eyes.

Arlen gave a yell and stumbled back, but Sandar was on him in an instant, knocking him to the ground. Flat on his back in heavy steel armor with another man atop him, Arlen had no way to rise.

"Ripping kill you!" he screamed, hammering Arlen about the head with heavy gauntleted fists. Rather than crippling him, the pain in his leg seemed to give him a mad strength like a cornered nightwolf.

Arlen's head felt like the clapper from a bell, and it was impossible to think clearly. Half-blind from the grit, he felt more than saw the long knife that suddenly appeared in one of Sandar's fists. The first thrust skittered across his breastplate, and the next bit into the interlocking rings at his shoulder joint.

Arlen threw his head back and howled. The armor turned the edge, but the pain was incredible, and he knew his shoulder would ache for days.

That was, assuming he lived through the next few minutes.

Sandar gave up trying to pierce the armor and stabbed the knife at Arlen's throat. Arlen caught his wrist, and they struggled silently for the next few moments. Arlen strained every muscle he had, but Sandar had weight and leverage in addition to his mad strength. The blade drew ever closer to the thin but vulnerable seam between Arlen's neckplate and helmet.

"Almost there," Sandar whispered.

"Not quite," Arlen grunted, punching a mailed fist into Sandar's broken knee. The Messenger screamed and recoiled in agony, and Arlen punched him full in the jaw, rolling as the man fell and reversing the pin. He pinned the knife arm with his knee, and landed several more heavy blows before the weapon fell from Sandar's limp hand.

WELL AFTER DARK, Arlen sat by the edge of the wardnet, watching One Arm and holding the thunderstick thoughtfully. In his other hand, he held the white-tipped match. His fingers itched to light it, and his other arm tensed, ready to throw. He pictured One Arm catching the stick in its jaws, and the explosion blowing the demon's head apart. Pictured its headless body lying on the ground, oozing ichor.

But he kept hearing Curk's voice in his head. *Them sticks ent ours, boy.* Curk might have been a coward in the end, but he was right about that. Arlen was no thief. He glanced at Sandar, surprised to find the man awake and staring at him.

"Know what you're thinking," Sandar said, "but there's a lot of loose rock up mountain. Thunderstick's more likely to cause a landslide than kill that demon."

"You don't know what I'm thinking," Arlen said.

Sandar grunted. "Honest word," he agreed. "Been trying to figure out why you splinted my leg and put a cold cloth on my head when I'd've killed you dead and tossed you off a cliff."

"Don't want you dead," Arlen said. "You can still sit a horse with that splint. You go back peaceful, and I'll tell Malcum just enough so your license is all you lose."

Sandar barked a laugh. "Ent Malcum I'm worried about, it's Count Brayan. He gets wind I tried to rob him, and my head'll be on a pike before the sun sets."

"If the shipment gets through, I'll see to it you keep your head," Arlen said.

"You'll forgive me if I don't trust that," Sandar said.

Arlen shrugged. "Try and kill me again tonight if you're up to it, but I warn you, I'm a light sleeper. Cross me again and I'll break enough bones so you never sit a horse again, then drag you up to Brayan's Gold with me to look the people you tried to rob in the eye."

Sandar nodded. "Sleep easy, I'll go back peaceful. Curk was right. You got a death wish, boy. Seen it before. Odds are you won't live long enough to tell anyone anything."

ARLEN HAD ALREADY broken camp by the time the demons sank back down into the Core in the pre-dawn light. He and Sandar left the wardstone and parted ways as the sun crested the mountainside.

The temperature grew colder as he ascended the winding mountain path. Spring was on in full on the Milnese plain, but here patches of snow were still visible, and his armor no longer seemed so warm with the wind chilling the steel. He began walking for long periods each day, as much to keep his blood flowing as to take some of the load off Dawn Runner, valiantly doing the work of two horses. They moved slower as a result, but there were still hours left before dark when Arlen reached the next of Brayan's great wardposts. He kept on, and camped at dusk behind his own circles. The following day he came upon the next post early, and the fourth right at dusk, making camp in its shelter.

The trail grew steeper, trees turning stunted and vegetation sparse amidst the rock and snow. The trail meandered, the never-ending wagon ruts skirting for miles around obstacles that had been too great for the trailblazers to cut or dig through. But still they climbed, and the weather grew colder. The ruts became indentations in the snow, and the trees vanished entirely.

He ceased trying to pass Brayan's wardposts, so tired by day's end that he was glad of their protection, though he often had to sweep the snow from them to restore full potency.

On his seventh day out from Miln, Arlen spotted the waystation Malcum had promised, far up the slope. It was a small structure, barely a hut, but after days of freezing cold, biting wind, and loneliness, Arlen was more than ready for a night indoors with someone to talk to.

"Ay, the station!" he cried, his call echoing off the stone facing above.

"Ay, Messenger!" a call came echoing back a moment later.

It was still the better part of an hour before Arlen reached the station, built into the side of the mountain. The warding on the building wasn't elegant, but it was thorough, and contained many wards Arlen was not familiar with. He took out his journal to quickly sketch them.

The station keeper, a yellow-bearded man wrapped in a heavy jacket lined with nightwolf pelt and bearing Count Brayan's arms came out to greet him. He was young, perhaps twenty winters, and carried no weapon. He strode right up to Arlen, extending a gloved hand to shake.

"You're not Sandar," he said, smiling.

"Sandar broke his leg," Arlen said.

"There's a Creator, after all," the man laughed. "I'm Derek of the Goldmen."

"Arlen Bales of Tibbet's Brook," Arlen replied, gripping the hand firmly.

"So you know what it's like to live at the end of the world," Derek said. "I want to hear all about it." He clapped Arlen's shoulder. "Coffee's hot inside, if you want to go

warm up. I'll stable your horse and stow the cart." It was only midday, but there was no question that Arlen would stay the night. Derek seemed as desperate for someone to talk to as Arlen.

"I'm warm enough to see the cargo stowed." Arlen said, though his feet and hands ached from the cold, and he could no longer feel his face. After what happened with Sandar, he didn't intend to let the crates of thundersticks out of his sight until they were under lock and key.

Derek shrugged. "You're free to suffer as you like." He took Dawn Runner's bridle and led the way to a pair of wooden barn doors embedded in the rock face of the mountain.

"Quickly, now," Derek said, as he grasped the great iron ring hanging from one of the doors, "don't want to let the heat escape." He opened the door just enough to admit the cart, and Arlen quickly led Dawn Runner through. There was a moment of sweet warmth, but then an icy wind roared in through the door as Derek was pulling it shut behind them, stealing the comfort.

Shivering, Arlen found himself in a small chamber, walled at the far end with a curtain of thick, ragged furs. Oil lamps flickered on either wall.

Derek took a lamp and drew the curtain aside to allow them passage. Arlen gaped. The entryway was just an alcove at the far end of a vast chamber, cut deep into the mountainside. It was filled with pens to handle teams of animals, granaries for their feed, and stowing area for a dozen carts. It was mostly empty now, but Arlen could well imagine the bustle and energy that ran through this great room when a caravan was passing though.

By the time the cart and horse were stowed, Arlen was sweating in his armor again. He looked about the great chamber, but there was no sign of a furnace vent or fire.

"Why's it so warm in here?" he asked.

Derek led him to the stone wall and knelt, pointing to a swirling pattern of wards painted at about knee height along the wall in either direction.

Arlen studied the pattern. It wasn't complex, but it was brilliant. "Heat wards. So the corelings attack the station doors outside…"

"And their magic gets leeched in here to warm the walls," Derek finished. "Some nights it gets hot as fire-spit, though. Almost rather be cold." Arlen, stifling in his armor, understood completely.

They took a side door out of the chamber and into the station itself. The ceiling, walls, and floor were the living stone of the mountain, cut into long halls, doorways and chambers. Heat wards ran along the base of the walls here, too.

"Didn't realize the station went back so far into the mountain," Arlen said.

"Nowhere else to go without blocking the road, and that's narrow enough," Derek said. "That pine lodge is just the front porch. Come on, I'll show you your chamber."

"Thanks," Arlen said. "If I don't get out of this ripping armor soon, I'm going to melt. Been sleeping in it a week now."

"Smells like it," Derek said. "You can have the royal chamber, seeing as how there's no one else here to take it. There's a tub."

The royal chamber was meant to allow Count Brayan and his heirs the luxury they were accustomed to when they went to inspect the mines. The chamber was very fine, filled with oak furniture, fur rugs, and heat warded stones. Most importantly, there was a proper bed, with a feathered mattress.

"The sun shines at last," Arlen said.

"Tub's over there," Derek said, pointing to a smooth depression in the stone floor beneath a heavy pump. "Pump's attached to a heated reservoir. Soak as long as you like and then come out for supper."

Arlen nodded, and the keeper left. He meant to take his armor off and get in the bath, but he fell back on the mattress for a moment, savoring its soft support, and found he didn't have the strength to rise. He closed his eyes, and fell dead asleep.

ARLEN EVENTUALLY MADE it out of his armor and over to the bath. Working the pump to fill the tub woke him back up, but the hot soak threatened to put him right out again. It was only the insistent growl of his stomach that made him pull on his clothes and stumble out of his room, feeling practically weightless without his armor.

"Derek?" he called.

"In the kitchen!" he heard the keeper reply. "Follow your nose!"

Arlen sniffed the air, and the growl in his stomach became a roar. His nose led him swiftly to the kitchen, where he found Derek wearing an apron and thick leather gloves as he bustled about.

"Sit," the keeper told Arlen, pointing to the closest stool at an oval table at the room's center, large enough for a score of men to eat at once. "Supper will be ready in a moment. You feeling human again?"

Arlen nodded as he sat. "It's only now that I'm clean, I realize just how filthy I was."

Derek went to a keg, filling a mug with foaming ale. He slid it across the polished table to Arlen with practiced ease. "Keep the kegs out in the snow till they're needed. Tapped this one special for you." He took his own mug and raised it in toast.

Arlen raised his in reply, and they both drank deeply. He looked at his cup in sudden surprise. "Might be a week on the road talking, but I'd swear that's Boggin's Ale."

"All the way from Tibbet's Brook," Derek agreed, taking Arlen's mug and putting a fresh head on it. "There are benefits to knowing every Messenger, wagon driver, and caravan guard by name."

"Boggin's was the first ale I ever drank," Arlen said, taking another swallow and letting it slide slowly over his tongue. Suddenly, he was twelve years old again, listening to Ragen and Old Hog haggling at the General Store in Tibbet's Brook.

"Nothing's better than your first," Derek said.

Arlen nodded, drinking again. "My life changed forever that day."

Derek laughed. "You and every other man." He set his mug down to take hollowed loaves of hard bread and fill them with a thick meat and vegetable stew.

Arlen fell on the meal like a coreling, tearing chunks of the warm crust and using them to scoop the delicious stew into his mouth. In minutes, he had scraped the plate clean down to the last crumb and speck of gravy. No meal in his life had ever been so satisfying.

"Night, even my mam never cooked like that," he said.

Derek smiled. "Ent got much else to do out here, so I've become a fair hand in the kitchen." He cleared the plates and ale mugs, replacing them with coffee cups. The brew smelled amazing.

"We can take the coffee out on the porch and watch the sunset, if you like," Derek said. "Got big windows made of that new warded glass they started making a couple years ago. You ever seen that?"

Arlen smiled. He was the one who had brought the glass wards to Miln, and Cob's shop did all Count Brayan's glasswork. He had probably warded the panes himself.

"I've heard of it," he said, not wanting to deflate the keeper, who looked quite proud.

As they left the kitchen, the stone floor became smooth pine boards, and they came to a large common area with fine pillowed benches and low tables. Arlen's eyes were immediately drawn to the window, and he gasped.

He had once thought the view of the mountains from the roof of the Duke's Library in Miln was the grandest in the world, but it was only a fraction of the view from the way-station, which seemed to tower over the mountains themselves. Far below, clouds swirled, and when they parted, he could see the tiny speck of Fort Miln, far, far below.

They sat by the windows, and Derek produced a pair of pipes and a weed pouch, along with a drybox of matches. For a short while, they smoked and drank their coffee in silence, watching the sun set from the top of the world.

"Don't think I've ever seen anything so beautiful," Arlen said.

Derek sighed, sipping his coffee. "Used to think so, too, but now it's just the fourth wall of my prison."

Arlen looked at him, and Derek blushed. "Sorry. Don't mean to steal the sight from you."

Arlen waved the thought away. "Honest word, I know how you feel. How often do they relieve you?"

"Used to be one month off and one on," Derek said, "but then I got caught in an abandoned shaft with the Baron's daughter over the winter, and he nearly had my stones cut off. Said he'd be corespawned before his daughter married a Servant. Been stuck out here three months now with no relief. Reckon she must've bled by now, else they would've called me back and fetched a Tender. I'll be lucky if they let me come home when the station closes for the winter."

"You've been alone here for three months?" Arlen asked. The thought was maddening.

"Mostly," the keeper said. "Messenger comes every fortnight, give or take, and caravans come a few times a year. Weeks on my arse, and then suddenly I've got a dozen wagons and fifty head of cattle and pack animals to manage, along with thirty guards needing quarter and a Royal to shout at me as I tend them."

"Was she worth it?" Arlen asked.

Derek chuckled. "Stasy Talor? Ent no girl in the world finer, and you can tell her I said so. I could just as easily have ended up the Baron's son-in-law instead of exiled out here."

"Can't you quit?" Arlen asked. "Find some other work?"

Derek shook his head. "There's only one work in Brayan's Gold, and that's what the baron gives you. If he says spend all year at the waystation, well..." he shrugged. "Still, I reckon talking to myself all day is better than swinging a pick in a dark mine shaft, worrying about cave-ins or digging too deep and opening a path to the Core."

"I don't think it works that way," Arlen said.

"Looks safer than Messaging, too," Derek said. "What happened to your cheek?"

Arlen reached up on reflex, running his fingers lightly over the wound where the bandit's arrow had pierced his cheek. He had treated it with herbs before stitching and it was healing well enough, but the flesh around the wound was an angry red and crusted with blood, obvious to anyone at a glance.

"Got hit by bandits after the thundersticks," he said. "Just past the third caravan wardpost." He quickly told the tale.

Derek grunted. "You got stones like a rock demon, waving a thunderstick around like that. Lucky they weren't looking to hurt anyone. A bad winter can put some folk past caring."

Arlen shrugged. "I wasn't giving up the cargo on my first real Messenger run without a fight. Sets a bad precedent."

Derek nodded. "Well, you ent likely to find any bandits the rest of the way. You'll be in Brayan's Gold the evening after next."

"Why so long?" Arlen said. "Aren't we almost at the top? Figure I can crack the whip and make it the rest of the way before late afternoon."

Derek laughed. "Air gets thin up there, Messenger. Just going up the cart path will have you laboring for breath like you were scaling the rock face. Even I feel tired for a couple of days when I go home, and I was born there."

By then, the sun was only a thin line of fire on the horizon, and a moment later, it winked out, leaving them in near-darkness for the rising. Outside, the whiteness of the snow resisted the darkening sky.

Arlen turned to Derek, who was little more than a silhouette. The bowl of his pipe glowed softly as he pulled at it. "Aren't you going to light any lamps?"

Derek shook his head. "Just wait."

Arlen shrugged and turned his attention back to the window, watching a rock demon rise on the road outside. It was the same slate color as those lower on the mountain, but smaller still, with long, spindly arms and legs with two joints. Sharp bits of horn jutted along its limbs, and it walked as much on all fours as it did upright.

"Always expected rock demons got bigger, the higher up you go," Arlen said. "Don't know why."

"Opposite's true," Derek said. "Less to hunt up here, and the deep snow trips up the big ones."

"That's good to know," Arlen said.

The rock demon caught sight of them and launched itself at the window with frightening speed. Arlen had never seen a rock move so fast or leap so far. It struck the ward-net in midair, and magic flared like lightning, throwing the demon back onto the road and almost pitching it down the mountainside. The coreling caught itself just in time, long talons catching fast in the rock at the cliff's edge.

Suddenly, all the wards at the front of the station came to life, flaring in succession as the magic leeched from the rock demon activated the wardnet, the pattern of symbols dancing across the walls and beams.

Many of the wards winked out soon after flaring, but Arlen could feel the heat wards still radiating faintly, and interspersed through the net and room were light wards, glowing with a soft, lingering luminescence.

Another coreling came at the window, a wind demon that shrieked as it dove from the sky. The net flared again, and the heat wards grew warmer as the light wards grew brighter. More corelings came at the window, and within a few minutes, the room was brighter than a dozen lamps might have made it, and warmer than if it had a roaring fire.

"Amazing," Arlen said. "I've never seen warding like this."

"Count Brayan spares no expense on his own comfort," Derek said. A demon suddenly struck the wards right in front of him, and he jumped, then scowled and made an obscene gesture at the offending demon.

"They always come at the window," Derek said. "Same demons, every night. I keep thinking one night they'll just give up, but they never learn."

"Seeing you makes them crazed," Arlen said. "Corelings might eat what they kill, but I think it's the kill itself that feeds them, human kills most of all. If they know you're here, they'll come and test the wards every night, even if it takes a hundred years for one to fail."

"Night, that's no comfort," Derek said.

"We're not meant to be comfortable, so long as night reigns," Arlen said, looking back out the window. "Is it just rock and wind demons up this high, then?"

"And snow demons," Derek said. "They rise even higher, where the snow never melts, but they'll drift down in a winter storm."

"You've seen snow demons?" Arlen asked, gaping at him.

"Oh, sure," Derek said, but under Arlen's glare, his expression grew less confident. "Once," he amended. "I think."

"You think?" Arlen asked.

"Window was foggy from the heat wards," Derek admitted.

Arlen raised an eyebrow, but Derek only shrugged. "I'm not looking to spin you some ale story. Maybe I saw one, maybe I didn't. Don't matter. I ent gonna stop drawing the wards. Jongleurs say that's what did us in, the first time. I'll keep drawing wards even if I never see a coreling again so long as I live. Tell my kids and grandkids to do the same."

"Honest word," Arlen agreed. "Will you teach me the snow wards?"

"Ay, I've some slate and chalk over there," Derek said, pointing. He tapped out his pipe as Arlen fetched the items, handing them to Derek and looking on eagerly as he drew.

He was surprised to see that the basic ward of forbidding for snow demons was an alteration of the water demon ward—lines flowing out to make the ward look almost like a snowflake. Derek continued to draw, and Arlen, a skilled Warder, quickly saw how the energy would move through the net. His hand moved of its own accord, inscribing perfect copies and notes in his journal.

Arlen was back in the feathered bed when One Arm tracked him to the station. He heard the demon's keening clearly, and the thunderous cracks as it tested the wards. The station was well protected, but with the giant rock demon powering the heat and light wards, the room grew continually hotter and brighter until it seemed he was standing in the sun at noon on a cloudless summer day in Soggy Marsh. Arlen lay bathed in sweat, the steam filtering in from the yard making everything damp. He would be sanding rust from his armor for days when he got home.

Finally, when sleep seemed impossible, he got up and began inscribing Derek's snow wards into his portable circles until morning. Derek was unable to sleep either, and had the cart hitched and ready to go. Arlen was on his way the moment the sun touched the mountainside.

As the keeper had warned, the going was much harder now. The cold of the road was welcome at first after the stifling heat of the station, but it wasn't long before the chill crept back into his bones, especially with his cloak and underclothes damp. An icy rime soon built up on his breastplate, and try as he might, Arlen could not seem to draw a full breath. Even Dawn Runner wheezed and gasped. They moved at a crawl, and though it had only been a few miles, they came to the next wardpost late in the day. Arlen had no desire to press on further.

The next day was harder still. His lungs had started to grow accustomed to the altitude overnight, but the trail continued to climb.

"There must be a lot of gold up there," Arlen told Dawn Runner, "to make this trip worth it." He immediately regretted the statement, not for lack of truth, but because the simple act of speaking aloud burned his lungs.

There was nothing for it but to press on, so Arlen put his head down and ignored the biting wind and drifts of powdery snow that came up to his knees in places. The wagon ruts vanished and the trail became all-but invisible, though markers were hardly needed. There was only one passable direction, bounded by the mountainside and a sheer cliff.

By afternoon, Arlen's entire body burned for lack of air, and the weight of his armor was unbearable. He would have taken it off, but he feared that if he stopped to do so, he might never get his legs to start walking again.

Plenty of folk make this trip, he reminded himself. *Ent nothing they did you can't do too.*

It was late in the day, with both Arlen and Dawn Runner on their last legs, when the small mining town came into sight. Brayan's Gold was a mixture of semipermanent structures, some of wood, and others built from the detritus of the mines, packed dirt and cut or pulverized stone. Most of the structures were poor; having tanned skins for doors and extensions made from tents, but there was a great wooden inn at the town's center, dominating the plateau.

Some few people moved about, women and children mostly, the men likely at work in the mines. Arlen wet his dry and cracked lips, putting his Messenger horn to them and blowing a long, clear note. The act sent knives of ice down his throat.

"Messenger!" a boy called. A moment later, Arlen was surrounded by children, jumping up and down and asking what he had brought them.

Arlen smiled. He had done the same when he was a boy and the Messenger came to Tibbet's Brook. He'd come prepared, and tossed sugar candies wrapped in twists of corn husk, small toys, and puzzles to the children. Their joy washed over him like a hot bath. Suddenly, climbing the mountain did not seem such an ordeal, and he found some of his strength returning.

"I want to be a Messenger some day," a boy declared, and Arlen ruffled his hair, slipping him an extra candy.

"You're a day early," someone said, and Arlen turned to see a small man dressed in a fine wool coat, his suede boots and gloves trimmed in white ermine fur. Behind him were two burly guards with small pick mattocks hanging from their belts that looked as much weapon as tool. The man approached with a genial smile, extending his hand.

"Ran into some bandits," Arlen said, shaking the hand. "Pressed ahead and skipped a wardpost to get some distance."

"Talor," the man introduced himself, "Count Brayan's cousin, and Baron of Brayan's Gold. What happened to Sandar?"

"Broke his leg," Arlen said. "I'm Arlen Bales."

Talor put his hand on Arlen's shoulder, leaning in close. "I'll tell you the same three things I tell every Messenger on his first run here. The climb is always hardest the first time, you'll catch your breath by morning, and it's easier going down than coming up." He laughed as if it were some great joke, and slapped the back of Arlen's armor with a clank.

"Still, I'm surprised they sent a first-timer here alone," Talor said.

"Had Messenger Curk with me, but he turned tail when the bandits hit," Arlen said.

Talor's eyes narrowed. "The shipment is intact?"

Arlen smiled. "Down to the last crate-nail." He handed over a wax-sealed tube pressed with Count Brayan's pick and hammer sigil as well as Curk's and his own seals.

"Ha!" the baron barked, his sudden tension gone. He slapped Arlen hard on the back. "This sounds like a tale for inside where it's warm!"

Talor raised a hand and his guards took the cart. Arlen walked beside him as he popped the seal on the tube and took out the manifest, his eyes running across the lines listing every item on the cart, down to the last letter and personal package. There was a personal letter from the count included in the tube, but Arlen was not privy to its contents. The baron stuffed the unopened envelope in his jacket pocket.

They came to the stable, where boys were unhitching Dawn Runner as the guards unloaded the cart. Arlen moved to help, but Talor put out a hand to hold him back.

"You just spent a week and more on the road, Messenger. Let the Servants handle the back bending." He handed the manifest to one of the stable guards and led the way inside.

LIKE THE WAYSTATION, the inside of the inn was heat warded and quite warm. At its front was a general store, the only resource in town for the necessities of life. Shelves behind the counter were filled with various tools and implements on sale, and chalked slates listed prices for food, livestock, and specialty items.

The room was crowded with women, many with children at their skirts as they called to the women taking orders and coin at the counter, who then called stocking instruction to more of Baron Talor's burly guards.

After the silence of the road, the din was overwhelming, but the baron quickly led the way through to the taproom in back and a quiet alcove with a richly appointed table. The bartender immediately brought them coffee.

Arlen blew on his steaming cup and sipped, the warmth beginning to seep back into his bones. The baron gave him time to take his ease until two women approached the table, one young, and another much older. Their dresses were plainer than Royal ladies favored in Fort Miln, but the fine cut and cloth still marked them.

Arlen stood politely as the baron kissed the women and turned to make introductions. "Messenger Arlen Bales, may I present my wife, Lady Delia Talor, and my daughter, Stasy."

Arlen noted the lack of the title "Mother" before the baroness' name, but he made no comment, bowing and kissing hands just as Cob had taught him.

The baroness was in her late fifties and no beauty, with a pinched face and a long neck, making her seem like a fishing bird. Stasy Talor, however, was all that Derek had claimed.

She was of an age with Arlen, with dark hair and blue eyes, tall and lithe in the Milnese way. She was pretty of face, but Arlen thought it was the sad cast to her eyes that made her truly beautiful. The lacings of her bodice were undone, as if the dress no longer fit well.

Reckon she must've bled by now, Derek had said, but suddenly Arlen wasn't so sure. He had to force his eyes up to meet hers before he was caught staring.

They all sat, and the baron and baroness leaned in close as they broke the seal and read Count Brayan's private letter. They began whispering harshly to one another and glancing at Stasy, but Arlen affected not to notice. He turned to the girl, hoping to engage her in conversation, but the baron's daughter did not acknowledge him, watching the discussion with her sad eyes.

Finally, the baron grunted and turned back to Arlen. "We'll soon be sending a caravan to Miln, so you can leave the cart here and head back with your horse alone. There will only be a handful of letters for your return."

Arlen nodded, and soon after a rich lunch was served. The baron and his wife kept up a constant flow of questions, asking for news from Miln, and Arlen dutifully recited every going on of note in the great city, along with whatever gossip he had overheard around the Messengers' Guildhouse. It was the gossip the Royals in exile seemed to covet most of all. Stasy took no part in the conversation, her eyes on her lap.

At last, a guard came over to the table with a chalked slate and the manifest. "There's a thunderstick missing." He eyed Arlen suspiciously.

"Nonsense," Talor said. "Count them again."

"Counted twice," the guard said.

The baron scowled, and his eyes flicked to Arlen for just an instant. His smile was forced. "Count a third time," he told the guard.

Arlen cleared his throat. "No, he's right. The missing stick's in front, tucked under the seat. I used it to scare my way past the bandits." He tried to tell himself he had forgotten the stick was there, but he knew deep down that he had left it there on purpose, hoping that perhaps no one would notice it was missing from the crate.

Everyone looked at him in shock. Even Stasy's eyes came up. Arlen quickly explained his encounter with the bandits, though he made no mention of Sandar.

Still, Baron Talor's mouth fell open with the telling. "You bluffed your way through by waving a thunderstick?"

Arlen smiled. "Never said I was bluffing."

Talor barked a laugh, and shook his head. "Not sure if that's the bravest or the craziest thing I ever heard! If it's true, you've got stones like a rock demon."

"They say a man doesn't become a Messenger unless he does," the baroness purred, giving Arlen a look that made him shudder. "But how did they find out about the shipment? Only Mother Cera and I knew the exact date."

"And Sandar," Arlen said, "who supposedly broke his leg the morning of."

"That's a big accusation, Messenger," Talor said, a quiet danger to his voice. "Have you any proof?"

Arlen knew his next words could mean life or death for Sandar. He shrugged. "Not accusing anybody. I'm just saying that if I was you, I'd get myself a new Messenger."

"How do we know you aren't just trying to get the job yourself?" the baroness asked.

"I'm just an apprentice," Arlen said. "Guild won't give me the job regardless."

"Bah," the baroness waved dismissively. "We could change that with a flick of a pen, and you know it. If you're telling the truth, we owe you a great debt."

Arlen nodded. "'Preciate that, milady, but I got an eye to see the world a bit before I settle on a regular run."

The baroness tsked. "You young ones always do, but one day you may not think steady work on a familiar path such a bad thing."

AFTER LUNCH, THE baron and the baroness stood. Arlen quickly got to his feet as well, and Stasy followed, her eyes still hollow.

"You'll have to excuse us," Talor said, "but we have some business to attend. Stasy will see you assigned a room and have the boys prepare supplies for your return. Compliments of Count Brayan, of course."

They vanished in a swirl of expensive fur, and Stasy gave a shallow curtsey. "Daughter Stasy, to serve you," she mumbled.

"You make it sound like a death sentence," Arlen said.

Finally, the baron's daughter met his eyes. "I apologize, Messenger, but the letter you brought from the count may as well have been." Her tone was the resigned one of someone whose tears are long dried.

"My legs still ache from the climb," Arlen said, gesturing to the table. "Will you sit with me a little longer?"

Stasy nodded and allowed Arlen to pull her chair. "As you wish."

Taking his own seat across from her, Arlen leaned over the table, his voice low. "They say if you whisper a secret to a Messenger, it's safer than a Tender's ear. No man, nor all the demons of the Core, can pull it unwilling from his lips, save the one it's meant for."

"This from the man who spread court gossip to my parents for the last hour." Stasy noted.

Arlen smiled. "Once those rumors reach the main hall of the Messengers' Guild, they are no longer secret, but I will tell you something that is."

Stasy raised an eyebrow. "Oh?"

"Derek still thinks there ent no woman finer than Stasy Talor, and prays you haven't bled," Arlen said. "Said I could tell you so."

Stasy gasped and put a hand to her chest. Her pale cheeks turned bright red and she looked around guiltily, but there was no one to see. She met his eyes fully now.

"Clearly I haven't," she said, absently touching the loose lacing about her belly. "But it makes no difference. He is not good enough for me."

"Are those your words, or your father's?" Arlen asked.

Stasy shrugged. "What does it matter? My father might have taken the 'i' from his name when mother died and he married Count Brayan's Royal cousin, but amongst the other nobles, he still feels like a Merchant, because his access to Royal circles is only as strong as his marriage vows. He wants better for me, and that means bearing children to a proper Royal husband and attending the Mothers School."

Arlen resisted the urge to spit on the floor. His father had tried to force him into an arranged marriage when he was eleven, and he remembered how it felt.

"Ent got anyone calling themselves Royal where I come from," he said. "Reckon we're better for it."

"Honest word," Stasy agreed sadly.

"How will your father arrange that, once your state is known?" Arlen asked.

Stasy laughed mirthlessly. "Likely he won't be able to, which is why that 'caravan' he's sending will ship me off to Count Brayan's Court to have my babe in secret amongst the Servants, at which point Countess Mother Cera will present me at court as having just arrived in the city and broker me a 'proper' marriage. Derek will never even know he's a father."

"You'll have to pass the waystation," Arlen said.

"Won't matter," Stasy said. "A new keeper will be sent with us to relieve him, and he'll be on his way back up the mountain before he even knows I'm locked in the coach."

She looked around to make sure they were not being watched, then reached out and gripped Arlen's hand. He saw passion in her eyes, and a thirst for adventure. "But if Derek knew what was coming and had supplies hidden, he could sneak down the mountain instead of up. Even if father sent someone after us the moment Derek went missing, we'd have a week's lead. More than enough to find each other, sell my jewelry, and disappear into the

city. We could get married no matter what his station and raise our child together."

Stasy looked at him, her eyes burning. "If you'll tell him this, Messenger, with no word to any other or mark in your log, I will pay whatever you ask."

Arlen looked at her, feeling as protective as an elder brother. He would take her message for nothing, but he could not deny there was something he wanted. Something the baron's daughter might be able to arrange.

"I need a thunderstick," he said quietly.

Stasy snorted. "Is that all? I'll have half a dozen of them packed with your supplies."

Arlen gaped, shocked at how easy it had been, but it quickly melted into a smile.

"What do you need the stick for?" Stasy asked.

"Gonna kill a rock demon that's been following me," Arlen said.

Stasy tilted her head, studying him in that way people had, as if trying to determine if he were joking or simply mad. At last she gave a slight shrug and met his eyes. "Just promise you'll deliver my message first."

ARLEN TOOK AN extra couple of days to catch his breath while the Goldmen finished preparing their messages for his return trip. He still tired easily in the thin mountain air, but the effects bothered him less each day. He spent the time wisely, watching the miners put the new thundersticks to use. Everyone wanted the favor of the new Messenger, so they were quick to answer his questions.

After watching as they reduced a solid rock face into tons of rubble in an ear-splitting instant, Arlen knew the destructive power of the thunderstick had not been exaggerated. If anything in the world could penetrate One Arm's thick carapace, it was this.

At last all was in order, and on the third day he put his heavy armor back on and headed to the stables. His saddlebags were already packed with supplies, and in them, Arlen found a small box of thundersticks packed in straw, along with a sealed envelope addressed to Derek in flowing script.

As the Baron had promised, it was far easier going down the trail than coming up. He made it to the first wardpost early in the day and pressed on, making the station well before dusk. Derek came out to meet him.

"I've a special letter for you," Arlen said, handing him the envelope. The keeper's eyes lit up at the sight, and he held the unopened letter up to the sun.

"Creator," he prayed, "please let it be that she ent bled."

He tore the letter open excitedly, but as he read his smile faded and his face slowly drained of color, becoming as white as the snow around him. He looked up at Arlen in horror.

"Night," he said. "She's out of her corespawned mind. Does she honestly think I'm going to run off to Miln?"

"Why wouldn't you?" Arlen asked. "You just prayed to the Creator for this very thing."

"Sure, when I thought it would make me the Baron's son-in-law, not when it means a week and more alone with the corelings."

"What of it?" Arlen asked. "There're campsites the whole way, and you're a fine Warder."

"You know what the worst thing about being a keeper is, Messenger?" Derek asked.

"Loneliness?"

Derek shook his head. "It's that one night it takes to get home. Sure, you can tumble downhill to the station in a day, but going back up, you always have to stop at that corespawned wardpost." He shuddered. "Watching the corelings stalk with nothing between you but magic. Don't know how you Messengers do it. I always come home with piss frozen to my breeches. I ent ever even done it alone. My da and brothers always come out when I'm relieved, so the four of us can take turns at watch."

"Folk make the trip all the time," Arlen said.

"And every year, at least half a dozen of them are cored on the way," Derek said. "Sometimes more."

"Careless people," Arlen said.

"Or just unlucky," Derek said. "Ent no girl worth that. I like Stasy well enough, and she's a ripping good rut if you get her alone, but she ent the only girl in Brayan's Gold."

Arlen scowled. Derek's calm obstinance, producing excuse after excuse for his cowardice, reminded him of his father. Jeph Bales, too, had turned his back on wife and child when it meant spending a night out of walls, and it had cost Arlen's mother her life.

"You go back to Brayan's Gold without Stasy and your child, you ent half a man," he said, and spit on the ground.

Derek growled and balled a fist. "What's it to you anyway, Messenger? What do you care if I run off with the Baron's daughter or not?"

"I care because that girl and the babe she's carrying deserve better than a ripping coward," Arlen said, and then there was a flash behind his eyes as Derek punched him. He rolled with the blow, coming around to drive his steel-plated elbow hard into the keeper's kidney. Derek howled and doubled over, and Arlen's next swing took him full in the face, laying him out flat in the snow. Feelings long buried came roaring to the surface, and Arlen had to check himself against a desire to continue the beating. He got back on his horse. "Don't think I'll be staying," he told Derek as the keeper rolled up onto his elbow, shaking his head to clear it. "Rather spend a night alone with the corelings than behind warded walls with a man who'll turn his back on his own child."

THE TRAIL CLIMBED a ridge and then dropped steeply, leaving Brayan's Gold and the Waystation on the far side of the mountain. Arlen's bruised cheek throbbed dully in the cold, and his mood grew blacker as he went. It was not the first time he had underestimated a man and felt betrayed, nor would it likely be the last, but always it was for the same reason. Fear. Fear of the corelings. Fear of the night. Fear of death.

Fear's a good thing, his father used to say. *It keeps us alive.*

But as with so many things, his father had been wrong. Jeph Bales had taken his fear and embraced it so fully he was convinced it was wisdom. Allowing himself to be ruled by fear might have extended Jeph's years, but under its heavy yoke, Arlen doubted his father had ever truly lived.

I will respect the corelings, Arlen thought, *but I will never stop fighting them.*

An hour before sunset, he stopped and made camp, laying out his circles and hobbling Dawn Runner, making sure she was well blanketed. He glanced at the crate of thundersticks, and decided he could wait no longer. Not far back he had crossed a narrow pass that was perfect for his purposes. He took two spears, two thundersticks, and his shield, hiking back uphill. He soon found the pass, overlooked by an escarpment much like the spot Sandar had chosen to waylay him and Curk.

He headed up the trail a bit further, scattering small lacquered plates etched with light wards in the snow along the path One Arm was soon to come bounding down. He returned to the pass and climbed the escarpment, looking out eagerly over the trail as he waited for dusk.

Twilight came quickly, and the stench of the demons rose with their foul mist, seeping from the ground to pollute the surface. The demons were sparse here, but not three feet from Arlen, a rock demon began to form on the escarpment, a squat beast, with armor the same color as the stone.

Arlen knew the demon would not notice him until it was fully formed, but he did not run or prepare a circle. Instead he crouched, waiting for the demon to solidify. When it was fully opaque he rushed in, shield leading. There was a full elemental circle of protection etched around the shield's edge, and magic flared as Arlen reached the coreling, stopping him short and hurling the rock demon off the outcropping, clear over the side of the cliff face.

Arlen smiled as the demon's roar receded to a distant crashing. There was a crack, and a shelf of snow far below broke free, burying the coreling where it landed. He doubted a fall could ever do lasting harm to a rock demon, but he took pleasure in its rage all the same.

It was a clear night, and twilight gave way to moon and stars that cast a dim glow on the snow. Even so, he heard the distant rumble of One Arm's approach long before he caught sight of the giant rock demon.

He waited, match held in his shield hand and thunderstick in the other. His spears were stuck point-down in the snow, in easy reach. When the ward plates on the trail flared, filling the pass with light, Arlen struck his thumbnail against the match tip, lighting it with a pop. He touched the fuse of the thunderstick to the fire where it caught with a crackle. Immediately, he drew back his arm and threw, raising his shield and peeking over its edge.

One Arm stopped its charge, looking at the projectile curiously, but then its good arm whipped across, faster than Arlen would have imagined possible, to bat the stick away. It flew up out of sight before exploding with a force that shook the whole mountainside and knocked Arlen to one knee, his ears ringing. The bang echoed in the distance. One Arm was distracted for a moment, but seemed otherwise unaffected.

"Corespawn it," Arlen muttered as the giant demon turned its attention back toward him. He was thankful he had brought a spare.

Pulling out the second thunderstick, Arlen fumbled for a match as One Arm charged. He managed to light and throw the second stick, but again One Arm was quick, stopping short and this time catching the stick, pulling it in for a closer look.

Arlen ducked behind his shield as the thunderstick went off right in the demon's face. The night lit up with a roar, and the shockwave of heat and force bowled him over, nearly knocking Arlen from the escarpment. He fell flat and held on for dear life.

A moment later he laughed out loud and looked up, expecting to see half the demon's head blown off, but One Arm stood there unharmed.

"No!" Arlen screamed, as the demon roared and resumed its charge. "No! No! No!"

He took up one of his spears, drawing back and throwing hard. The missile struck the demon full in the chest, splintering on impact and doing no harm.

"What does it take to kill you?" Arlen cried, but the demon took no heed. Knowing the fight was lost, he cursed and dropped his shield to the ground, standing at the center of its small circle of protection.

But the ground shook from the demon's charge, a sound like constant thunder in the air, and Arlen's knees buckled. He stumbled from his perch atop the convex shield, and knew he could not trust its protection through the night.

Quickly, he picked his shield back up, taking a spear in his other hand. His armor might protect him long enough to retreat back to Dawn Runner's circle, but it was a long

way to run through the snow at night, especially with seventy pounds of steel on his back. The roaring filled his ears, and it seemed the whole mountain shook.

One Arm reached the outcropping, leaping up to catch its lip. The great talons of its good arm dug into the stone as it pulled itself up. Arlen stabbed at the hand uselessly as the roaring sound grew deafening, and suddenly he realized it wasn't One Arm causing it. He looked up and saw nothing but whiteness, rushing at him like water.

Barely thinking, Arlen leapt from the far side of the escarpment, half-sliding and half-tumbling down to the trail. Ignoring the sharp spikes of pain from the fall, he immediately fetched up against the mountainside and raised his shield.

Shaken loose by the thundersticks, the avalanche struck One Arm full on, knocking the giant demon over the cliff in much the same manner as Arlen had its smaller cousin. He saw the demon fall an instant before being buried himself.

There was surprising weight to the snow, and Arlen's arm threatened to buckle, but he succeeded in creating a pocket of shelter, and when the rumbling ceased, he was able to quickly dig himself out as the majority of the snow continued on down the mountainside.

He went over to the edge of the cliff, but there was no sign of One Arm in the darkness, nor sound of its cries. Arlen laughed again and pumped a fist into the air. Perhaps he had not been able to kill the demon, but he had faced it again and lived to tell the tale, and it might be days before One Arm found his trail again.

A low growl sounded off to the side, and the grin died on Arlen's face. The avalanche must have brought a demon down from higher up the mountain. His hand tightened on his spear, and he turned slowly, shield up.

The moon and stars were bright and reflected off the snow, casting a gray gloom through the darkness. At first he didn't see it, but as the coreling drew closer, the wards on his armor and shield began to draw upon its magic, glowing softly. There was movement in the wardlight, and finally Arlen caught sight of it, a demon with pure white scales that glittered like snowflakes. It looked much like a flame demon, no bigger than a mid-sized dog and crouched on all fours, with a long snout and horns that ran back flat over pointed ears and a long, corded neck.

On impulse, Arlen spat upon the demon, and was amazed to find the rumor was true. As his spittle struck the pure white scales, it froze and burst with a crack.

The snow demon's eyes narrowed, and its snout split wide in what might have been a smile. It made a horrid sound in its throat, and spat back at him.

Arlen managed to get his shield up in time, catching the spray. The surface turned white with rime, and his shield arm grew numb from the cold.

The demon leapt at him then, and his shield, made brittle by the coreling's coldspit, shattered on impact. Arlen was knocked onto his back in the snow, but managed to get a leg between the demon and himself, kicking it away. The snow demon was knocked to the cliff's edge, but dug in its front claws and held fast, back talons scrabbling for purchase. In a moment it would be back at him.

Arlen shook off the remains of his shield and charged the demon, spear leading. He meant to send it tumbling down to wherever One Arm had landed, but the coreling recovered faster than he anticipated. It tamped down and sprang to meet his charge.

Arlen spun his spear into a horizontal defense, but the coreling caught the shaft in its teeth and bit through the thick wood like it was a celery stalk. Arlen took the two halves and swung them like clubs to box the demon's ears, knocking it aside.

Before the demon could recover, he turned and ran. It was one thing to press an advantage when a demon was hanging by its claws, but another to fight one head on. There were no snow wards on his armor, and he had no defense against its coldspit.

The wards on his armor continued to glow softly, helping light his way, but also serving as a beacon to the snow demon and any other corelings that might be in the area. He stumbled through the snow, using the downward slope to add reckless speed to his flight.

But in the end, it was not enough. His legs sank into the loose snow, but the snow demon ran across its surface like a bug skating on water. He felt it hit his back, knocking the wind from him and bearing him to the ground.

Arlen rolled with the impact, shaking the demon off before it could find a seam in his armor, but he had barely rolled onto his back before it was upon him again. He put up his armored forearm to hold it back, and the demon caught the thick steel plate in its teeth and began to squeeze.

Metal squealed and bent, and though his arm was still numbed by the coldspit, Arlen howled in agony. The demon's talons raked at him, tearing easily through the steel mesh at his joints, and piercing the larger plates like blacksmith shears.

Arlen felt the cold claws pierce his flesh, like being stabbed with icicles, and screamed into the night. The demon thrashed its head from side to side, teeth still clamped, threatening to tear his arm clear out of the socket. Blood spattered his face from the injured limb.

But in that instant, sure of his own death, Arlen caught sight of the demon's bare belly, smooth like new snow, and saw a chance. With the fingers of his free hand he caught a swab of his own blood and reached out, drawing a crude heat ward on the snow demon's stomach.

Immediately, the ward flared, brighter and more powerful than any he had seen at the station. Those wards were powered by feedback alone, but this ward drew on the coreling's dark magic directly. Arlen felt his face burn from its power.

The demon shrieked and let go its grip, and Arlen shoved it away. It landed on its back, and Arlen saw his blood ward blacken the white scales, then burst into a flame that consumed the demon like sunlight. He was left panting in the snow, bloodied and torn, but very much alive as he watched the thrashing snow demon immolated in fire.

He stumbled quickly back to the campsite, breathing a great sigh of relief when he was once again within the safety of his circles. He needed a prybar to get some of the pieces of his armor off, but there was no choice, as the twisted metal cut off his blood flow in more than one place, and cut into his skin in others. He lit the fire he had wisely laid in advance, and spent the rest of the night huddled by it, trying to restore feeling to his arm as he stitched his flesh.

Feeling slowly returned to his numb arm, bringing with it a maddening pain as if he had been burned. But through it all, he was smiling. He hadn't killed the demon he set out to, but he had killed one nonetheless, and that was more than anyone he had ever known could claim. Arlen welcomed the pain, for it meant he was alive when he had no right to be.

Arlen led Dawn Runner down the steep trails the next morning, happy to walk and keep his blood pumping. Late in the day, there came a cry behind him.

"Messenger!"

Arlen turned to see Derek running hard after him. He stopped and the keeper soon caught up, stumbling to a stop. Arlen caught him with his good arm and set him to hang on Dawn Runner's saddle, red-faced and panting. His eye was blue and swollen where Arlen had punched him.

"You're a long way from the station," Arlen said, when the keeper caught his breath.

"Whole mountain heard those thundersticks in the night, and the slide that followed," Derek said. "I took my skis and went looking for you."

"Why?" Arlen asked.

Derek shrugged. "Figured either you were dead, and I should try and send your bones to your mother, or alive, and needing some help. You ent my favorite person, Messenger, but anyone deserves that much."

"That would have taken you to the site of the avalanche, six hours back," Arlen said, "where you would have seen my tracks, and known I was all right. Why keep on?"

Derek looked at his feet. "I knew you were right yesterday, about me not standing by my own. I think that's what got me so mad. Then when I saw what was left of the demon you killed, it was like a kick in the stones. Dunno what came over me, I just kept on going while my nerve held. Figure the caravan will think I'm dead, but they'll still have to get Stasy out of Brayan's Gold before her belly swells. I'll go to Miln and wait for her."

Arlen smiled and clapped him on the shoulder.

COB WAS BERATING one of the apprentices when Arlen returned to the shop. Arlen's master was always snappish when he was worried. He looked up at the door chime and saw Arlen standing there, Derek in tow. The irritation left his face, and the apprentice wisely used the distraction to vanish into the back room.

"You made it back," Cob grunted, heading to sit at his workbench without pausing for so much as a handshake.

Arlen nodded. "This is Derek, out of Brayan's Gold. He's got a steady warding hand, and could use some work."

"You're hired," Cob said, picking up his etching tool. He pointed his leathery chin at Arlen's left arm, missing its armor and bound in a sling. "What happened?"

"You now know someone who's met a snow demon firsthand," Arlen said.

Cob shook his head and laughed aloud, bending over his work.

"Should've known if they were out there, you'd find one," he muttered.